FOREVER SAM

BOOKS IN THE PUPPY PATROL SERIES ™

COMING SOON

PUPPY PATROL™

FOREVER SAM

JENNY DALE

Illustrations by Mick Reid
Cover illustration by Michael Rowe

AN
APPLE
PAPERBACK

SCHOLASTIC INC.
New York Toronto London Auckland Sydney
Mexico City New Delhi Hong Kong Buenos Aires

SPECIAL THANKS TO CHERITH BALDRY

ISBN 0-439-33801-8

12 11 10 9 8 7 6 5 4 3 2 1   3 4 5 6 7 8/0

Printed in the U.S.A.   40
First Scholastic printing, April 2003

CHAPTER ONE

"Jake, you silly dog!" Neil Parker called. "Come out of there!"

Dead leaves and clumps of grass flew into the air as the young Border collie burrowed into the bank. Neil watched him, laughing, while his younger sister Emily and Sam, Jake's dad, climbed the last few yards to the top of the hill.

Emily and Sam exchanged a glance, as if to say, "What's he up to now?" and Emily was sure that the older dog was grinning. "Have you found some rabbits, Jake?" she asked.

Jake flung himself out of the drift of leaves and tore off into the bushes, barking excitedly.

"Let him have a run," Neil said as he watched the

young dog disappear. "Sam can't keep up with him these days."

It was a warm late summer's day and a gentle breeze shook the scattered trees along the pathway. Neil used his sleeve to wipe the sweat off his forehead and brushed back his spiky brown hair.

While he waited for Jake to run the itch out of his feet, he stood looking back down the slope he had just climbed, toward the buildings of King Street Kennels, his home just outside the small country town of Compton. Neil and Emily's parents, Carole and Bob Parker, ran a boarding kennel and rescue center there. Dogs were everything in Neil's life and he wouldn't have it any other way. He loved the boarding dogs and the rescue dogs equally, but best of all were his Border collies, Sam and Jake.

The previous year, Sam had been diagnosed with a

heart problem, and since then he'd had to take life easy. On the other hand, young Jake was overflowing with energy. From an inquisitive puppy, he was now turning into a happy, outgoing youngster who kept Neil on the go from morning to night.

"When we get back," Emily said, "I want to plan my party. I've got to make a list of the guests and a list of food and a list of games we'll play. . . ."

Neil grinned. It was Emily's tenth birthday in two weeks, and she was already getting excited. And she loved making lists! "Do you know what Mom and Dad are getting you?" he asked.

Emily shook her head. "I asked Mom, but she said it was a surprise. And then she laughed." Emily's eyes shone. "I bet it's something *really* special!"

Neil agreed. His mom and dad were good at thinking up presents. He would have to think of something interesting to give Emily, too. All the same, he thought, if you lived at King Street with dogs all around you, what else could you possibly want?

He and Emily walked on slowly, with Sam at heel, catching glimpses of Jake every now and then, bounding through the undergrowth. Even when he was out of sight, little flurries of excited barking told them where he was.

"He's good at coming when he's called now," Neil said. "I'm teaching him —"

He broke off. From the trees just ahead, he heard the barking of a different dog, but he couldn't see it.

"Jake!" he called. "Jake! Here, boy!"

The young dog did not appear.

"So much for coming when he's called," said Emily.

"Jake!" Neil jogged on ahead to the clump of trees. He was getting closer to them, when there was a sudden frightened whimpering and Jake shot out of the undergrowth and scurried toward him. Another dog loped after Jake — a big mongrel with a reddish coat. It was still barking loudly.

Without thinking, Neil stepped between the two dogs. The mongrel halted and stood stiff-legged, growling.

Neil suddenly felt scared.

The dog looked rough and uncared for — and very wild. There was no sign of anyone who might have been its owner.

Neil heard Emily coming up behind him. Without taking his eyes off the mongrel, he said, "Em, hang on to Jake and Sam."

"But what about —"

"Do it!" Trying to sound as firm as his dad, he said to the mongrel, "Sit!"

The mongrel lowered its head, still snarling, its teeth bared. Neil took a step backward, and at that moment it leaped. Neil tried to dodge, but stumbled and fell. Before the mongrel could reach him, more furious barking broke out and a black-and-white streak threw itself onto the strange dog.

"Sam!" Emily cried out.

For a minute, Neil was winded. He could do nothing but stare at the tangle of legs and tails and snapping jaws as Sam and the mongrel fought, rolling over and over on the ground. Then he scrambled to his feet.

Emily was crouched beside Jake a yard or so away, firmly gripping his collar. "I couldn't hold him!" she gasped.

Neil gave a swift glance around. There was no sign of the mongrel's owner. He grabbed the end of a dead branch that lay in the grass; the other end was a bunch of twigs and dead leaves. He raked it across the two dogs, still locked together in combat, trying to separate them and block the mongrel as it fought to sink its teeth into Sam's flank.

He managed to maneuver the branch between them and thrust it at the mongrel's chest. Its feet scrabbled against the branch and Neil took a step forward, pushing harder. The mongrel fell back. "Sam! Down!" Neil shouted.

Sam lay on the turf panting as Neil advanced on the mongrel, shouting and holding the branch in front of him. He was so angry by now that he never even thought about whether it would launch another attack on him. "Get out! Go on!" he yelled. "Scram!"

For a few more paces, the mongrel kept on snarling,

and then it suddenly turned and bounded away, yelping, its tail between its legs. "Good riddance!" Neil shouted after it.

He kept holding the branch and watched the strange dog as it ran down the hill and disappeared into some bushes farther along. Neil hardly ever saw a dog he didn't like, but he felt scared and angered by this one. And there was still no sign of the owner — the one who was letting it run wild.

Neil threw the branch down and turned back to join Emily and the dogs.

Emily had released Jake, who came running to meet Neil as he walked back along the track. Emily was kneeling on the ground, bending over Sam. As she turned toward him, Neil saw that she looked white and frightened. He started to run.

"Neil . . ." Emily didn't need to say anything else.

Sam lay on his side. He was panting, fast and shallow, and his eyes were closed. Neil could see his flank moving rapidly up and down with his breath. Apart from that, the Border collie was motionless.

"Sam . . ." Neil knelt beside him and stroked his head. He tried to make his voice cheerful. "Come on, boy. It's all over. You were great."

"He just rolled over," Emily said. She sounded as if she was going to cry. "He wouldn't get up."

Jake came up and nosed Sam. Neil thought he looked puzzled and just as helpless as he felt himself. "Hey, Sam. Come on, boy," he said gently.

"Neil," said Emily, "you know Sam isn't supposed to overdo things. What if the fight was too much for him? What if . . . ?"

What if he's dying? Neil knew how she had meant to finish, but neither of them could put the thought into words. "He just needs to rest," he said. "He'll be fine. Em, why don't you take Jake home? We'll follow you down in a little while."

Emily looked at him solemnly. "I don't think you will," she said. "I'll go and get Dad."

It seemed like a lifetime before Emily came back with Bob Parker. Neil had never been so glad to see his dad.

Sam still lay on his side. His breathing had eased a bit, but he hadn't moved. Bob knelt beside him on the turf.

Neil's dad was a huge man, with brown curly hair and a beard. He ran his large, gentle hands over Sam, carefully checking him for injuries.

"I don't think he was bitten," said Neil.

"But I think the fight must have been more than he could take," said Bob. "I rang Mike Turner. He's coming right over. He'll be at the kennel by the time we get back with Sam. Let's get him home."

Hearing that, Neil became a little less desperate. Mike Turner, the Compton vet, had told Neil what to do when Sam first collapsed. Together they had monitored his health ever since. If anyone could help Sam now, Mike could.

Bob lifted Sam carefully in his arms and headed down the hill toward the kennel. Neil and Emily followed. Neil thrust his hands deep into his pockets, his fists clenched, and watched his feet. He couldn't talk or look at anyone in case he started crying.

When Neil and the others reached home, the vet was sitting at the big table in the kitchen, drinking a mug of tea. Carole Parker, Neil's mom, was spreading blankets on the floor, near the warm stove.

Mike got up as Bob made his way into the kitchen with Sam in his arms. "OK, let's have a look at him," he said.

"He got into a fight," Neil said, "with this strange

dog on the hill. And then he just collapsed." His panic started to overflow. *"Mike, you've got to do something!"*

"Take it easy, Neil," Bob said. "You know he'll do the best he can."

He carried Sam across the kitchen to the blankets and, as Bob laid him down, Sam raised his head a little, blinked, and lay still once again.

"He's coming around!" Neil exclaimed. "Hey, he's going to be fine!"

Bob drew him back so that Mike would have room to work. Reluctantly, Neil sat at the table, keeping a

hand on Jake's collar so the young dog wouldn't get in Mike's way, and followed every movement the vet made as he gently examined Sam.

While everyone was waiting for Mike's verdict, Bob asked, "What's all this about a strange dog?"

"It was vicious," Neil said. "A real brute. It just went for Jake, and then for me."

"Neil and Jake could have been badly hurt, if it hadn't been for Sam," Emily added. She was pink with indignation. "Nobody should let a dog run wild like that!"

"What did it look like?" Bob asked.

Neil described the reddish, mangy-looking mongrel. "It might be a stray," he said. "It didn't look cared for."

Bob thanked Carole for the mug of tea she put in front of him. "I haven't seen a stray dog up there recently," he said.

"Neither have I," said Carole. "Neil, Emily, don't go up there again by yourselves until we know a little more. I don't want you attacked again like that."

"I think we should tell Sergeant Moorhead," Emily said.

"Good idea," said her father. "He might have had some other reports about it, especially if it's attacked anybody else. I'll call him — no, we'll go and see him right after lunch."

"Yes, I want to —" Neil began, and broke off as Mike Turner squatted back on his heels, running a hand down Sam's glossy black-and-white flank. Sam seemed to be sleeping, his breathing quieter now. "Well?" Neil felt as if his voice didn't belong to him. "Is he going to be OK?"

Mike Turner's face was grave. "I'm sorry, Neil," he said. "This is going to be tough for you, I know. The trouble is . . . well, Sam wasn't hurt in the fight, but it put too much strain on his heart."

Neil stared at him. Mike had helped the Parkers with more problems and disasters than he could count, but Neil couldn't remember ever seeing the vet look this upset.

"He is . . . ?" Neil cleared his throat. "He is going to get better, isn't he?"

Mike shook his head. "Not this time, Neil. His heart just isn't strong enough. He's very tired and . . ." He stopped and swallowed. "I'm sorry. There's nothing I can do. I'm afraid Sam is going to die."

CHAPTER TWO

"**N**o!" Neil sprang to his feet, knocking his chair over. "Sam can't die! He can't!"

He dropped onto his knees on the blankets beside Sam and threw an arm across the sleeping dog, as if he could protect him.

Carole said, "Neil, don't . . ." and stopped, shaking her head helplessly.

Quietly, Emily started to cry.

Jake came nosing up to Neil, who put his other arm around the younger dog and hugged him tightly. He could feel tears starting to escape from his eyes. "I'm going to look after him," he said. "Anything he needs, he can have it."

"Mike, what do we do now?" Bob asked.

The vet stood up, rubbing his hands over his face

as if he was tired. "I hate this," he said. His voice was quiet, but fierce. "It's the one part of my job I really hate. With any sickly animal, there comes a time when there isn't anything more I can do, and I have to tell their owners. It makes me feel so useless."

"You're not being fair to yourself," Carole said. She tried to smile. "Without you, Sam could have died months ago."

Mike shook his head and let out a long breath. "Neil, I'll take Sam back to the clinic with me. I'll run a few tests, take another X ray, and then —"

"No!" Neil interrupted, looking up from the dogs.

"He's not going to die now, this minute, Neil. I promise you. It could be days, maybe even weeks . . ."

"Maybe not at all," Neil said.

"Don't get your hopes up," Bob said. "Let Mike do what he thinks is best."

"OK," said Neil. He gave Mike a suspicious stare. "You're not going to . . . ?"

It took a few moments before Mike understood what he was asking. "Put him to sleep? No, Neil, honestly. And if that does seem to be the best option to save him from pain . . ." He raised a hand as Neil seemed about to protest. "You'll be consulted, Neil. It'll be *your* decision."

"I'll never let you do that!" Neil wished he could keep his voice steady, but he couldn't.

"Not even if it's best for Sam?" Bob asked.

Neil looked down at his dog, his best and truest friend, and couldn't find the words to reply.

Mike left for the clinic with Sam in the back of his car.

Neil decided not to go with him. Sam was stable for the time being, and Mike promised to call if there was any change in his condition.

Carole went to get Sarah, Neil's five-year-old sister, from her ballet class, while Bob finished preparing lunch.

It was one of the most miserable meals Neil could remember having. Carole had warned him not to tell Sarah how serious Sam's condition was, and that meant no one could talk about it. In any case, Sarah guessed that something was the matter and sat in unnatural silence, picking the mushrooms out of her lasagna. For once no one scolded her; even Bob and Carole didn't feel like eating, and Neil just pushed his plate away after a few mouthfuls. He could hardly tear his eyes away from Sam's empty basket.

"OK," Bob said, when the meal was over. "Neil, Emily, we're going down to the police station. We'll have a word with Sergeant Moorhead about that stray."

Sergeant Moorhead was at the desk when the Parkers arrived at Compton Police Station. He made notes as Neil and Emily told the story of the stray dog up on the hill.

"Sounds nasty," he commented when they had finished. "A lot of families with children walk their dogs up there. I'll send somebody to have a look."

"If it is a stray," Bob said, "and you do find it, I suppose you'd better bring it to the rescue center."

Neil stared at his dad. He couldn't believe that Bob would suggest helping the dog who had attacked him and nearly killed Sam. Neil didn't want anything to do with it.

He didn't say anything. His earlier panic had subsided, but he felt like he had a tight knot in his stomach. He knew if he started to talk about what the mongrel had done to Sam he would start crying again — in the middle of the police station.

Sergeant Moorhead scratched his short, gray hair with the end of his pencil. "We'll see," he said. "If it has an owner, he might —"

The doors of the police station swung back sharply. A warm wind blew in, bringing with it Paul Hamley, the principal of Neil and Emily's school, and his nutty Dalmatian, Dotty.

"Sergeant . . ." He was panting and looked upset. He stopped when he saw the Parkers, and Dotty pulled to the end of her leash, putting her front paws on Emily's chest.

Emily laughed. "Down, girl! Sit."

Dotty sat. She had become much more obedient since Neil and Emily had first met her — though Neil hoped she would never lose her crazy unique

ways. In spite of everything, he couldn't help smiling when he saw her, bright-eyed and panting, her tongue lolling out in a doggy grin.

"Sorry, Bob," said Mr. Hamley breathlessly. "I didn't see you there. Sergeant, I've got something to report."

"It's a madhouse today," Sergeant Moorhead said, licking the end of his pencil and turning over a page in the incident book. "OK, Mr. Hamley, go ahead."

"It's the badgers," said Mr. Hamley. His voice was shaking with anger. "Someone's killed the badgers."

"What?" Emily looked up from petting Dotty. "Not the ones you watch, sir?"

Mr. Hamley nodded. "I'm afraid so, Emily."

"That's terrible," said Bob.

"Do you know the place I mean, Sergeant?" asked Mr. Hamley. "On the hill just on the edge of Priorsfield Farm. I've been watching that family for months. . . . Anyway, I took Dotty for a walk up there this afternoon, and . . ." He paused and shook his head. "Someone has dug the den out. There are three badgers, lying there, all dead. I felt sick when I saw them."

Neil knew how much Mr. Hamley loved his badgers. There was a display in Meadowbank School of photographs he had taken. He spent hours watching them with special night-vision binoculars.

"Who would do a thing like that?" asked Emily.

Sergeant Moorhead looked up from his writing. "A lot of farmers think badgers are pests. They don't like them on their land."

"But that den is on Harry Grey's land," said Bob Parker. "Harry wouldn't kill a badger."

The sergeant shrugged and went on with his notes.

"Hey, just a minute," said Neil. "The badger den isn't all that far away from where we saw that mongrel this morning. Do you suppose the same dog might have killed the badgers?"

"What mongrel is this?" Paul Hamley asked.

Bob quickly brought him up to date, but before he had finished Mr. Hamley was shaking his head. "I suppose a dog might kill badgers, but it would take somebody with tools to dig them out." He sighed heavily. "Somebody who wanted the badgers dead."

That evening, Neil was sitting at the kitchen table with his homework books spread out in front of him. He had a pen in his hand, but he hadn't written a word. He couldn't concentrate on social studies when he still didn't know what was happening to Sam.

At the other side of the table, Emily had finished her work and was packing her books away.

Looking up, Neil asked, "Emily, have you done the list for your party? Mom bought you some invitations yesterday."

"No, not yet," said Emily. "I'm not sure I want a party — not when —"

"Don't be silly," Neil interrupted gruffly. "You can't not have a party on your birthday. You'll be ten. Double digits. It's a big day."

Emily still looked uncertain but unearthed a pad of paper, anyway, and started to write down names. "Julie, of course, and Toby . . ."

Neil watched her, wishing he could take more interest and join in the fun of planning. He knew how much Emily had been looking forward to this birthday. But the image of Sam lying panting on the side of the path kept forcing itself back into his mind.

He threw the pen down and banged his homework book shut. There was nothing on his mind except

Sam, so what was the point of trying to do anything else?

The doorbell rang. "Neil, can you get that? I'll be down in a minute," his mom called from upstairs.

Neil pushed himself to his feet and went to answer it. Mike Turner was on the step. He had Sam sitting at his feet.

"Sam!" Neil's face broke into a wide grin. He squatted down and hugged the Border collie. "Hey, Sam, you're home!"

"Let's go inside," said Mike. "We need to have a talk."

Neil took one glance at his face, and the sudden hope that Sam was recovering vanished. Mike looked strained and tired. Without speaking, Neil led the way back to the kitchen, with Sam padding at his heels.

Bob and Carole were waiting in the kitchen, and as soon as Neil walked in, Emily left her list and sat on the floor beside Sam to welcome him home. Jake got up from his basket and nuzzled his dad. Mike sat heavily in one of the chairs by the table.

"I'm sorry, Neil," he said. "I haven't got any good news for you. The tests I did today just confirm what I told you earlier. I'm afraid he hasn't got very long."

Neil bit back a protest. There wasn't any point in protesting. All he could do was his very best for Sam and hope that somehow he could keep putting off the day when his time would run out. Carefully keeping his voice steady, he asked, "What can I do for him?"

Mike shrugged. "Just make him as comfortable as you can. He's not in any pain. Keep on with his usual medication, and give him gentle exercise if he seems to want it. There's no point stopping him from enjoying himself. He'll probably sleep a lot, but the more you can stick to his usual routine, the better. Let his last few days be as normal as possible."

Neil looked down at Sam. He was lying on the floor, his head raised as Emily rumpled his ears, but after a moment he let his muzzle drop onto his paws as if he was very tired. All the liveliness that Neil loved in him was gone.

"OK," Neil said. He bent down to stroke Sam. "You get a good rest, boy. We're all going to look after you."

When Mike had gone and Sam was asleep in his basket, Neil got out the album with all his photographs of Sam, a scrapbook of press cuttings, and the box that held his Agility certificates and ribbons. Sam had been a star performer and champion in several local Agility competitions before they found out about his heart condition.

Neil fished around in the box until he found the last ribbon of all, the red one Sam had won in a big Agility contest in Manchester the day he had first collapsed. Neil had accepted that there wouldn't be any more, but he knew now he had never accepted that Sam's life would come to an end.

He flipped open the album.

First, he saw some photos taken by Bob and Carole, when Neil was younger and Sam was younger. Then, the first ones Neil had taken himself, a bit out of focus, he had to admit, showing Sam as a happy young dog. And the latest ones that he had taken with Emily, photographs of Sam and Jake together. The album, the box, and the scrapbook held a record of all of Sam's life.

But two items were missing: Sam's pedigree and his registration certificate as a purebred dog. A few years ago, when Neil was only seven, Sam had been found near the old railroad tracks and brought to the Parkers' newly opened rescue center. No one had ever found out how Sam came to be abandoned or who his original owner had been. Neil was convinced that Sam had a good pedigree, but there was no proof.

He said to himself, "I wish I knew . . ."

"Knew what?" Bob asked.

Neil turned around and saw his dad come into the kitchen to wash out his mug in the sink.

"About Sam. I wish I had his registration papers. I want to know who he is."

Bob put down the dish towel and leaned back against the drain board. "He's your dog, Neil. Isn't that enough?"

"Yes . . . I don't know." Neil rested his elbows on

the table and his chin on his hands. "I want to know what happened, Dad. I want to know who would abandon a great dog like Sam."

"We've talked about this before, Neil," Bob said. "It's not realistic, after all this time, to —"

"It is!" Neil insisted. "It's got to be."

Sam trusted him, and in a strange sort of way Neil felt he would be letting him down if he didn't do all he could to find out the truth. Quietly, he said, "I've got to try, Dad, before Sam . . ." He broke off. A photo caught his eye. Sam was looking proudly at Jake playing in the sunshine on a warm spring evening. Neil felt real determination stirring within him. He was going to find out about Sam's past — no matter what anyone said.

CHAPTER THREE

Bob Parker sat down at the kitchen table opposite his son. Neil was afraid he was going to argue with him, but all Bob said was, "Tell me why it matters."

Neil didn't look at him. He started pushing Sam's ribbons around on the table, arranging them in a circle around the last red one.

Finally, he said, "It just does."

When Bob just waited quietly for him to speak again, he added, "I know Sam's a pedigree dog. You only have to look at him. He deserves to have his papers."

"It won't matter to Sam," Bob pointed out.

"But it will to me. And it will to Jake."

At the mention of his name, the young Border collie raised his head from where he was snoozing beside Neil's chair. Neil reached a hand down and stroked his head. "Because Sam hasn't got his papers," Neil went on, "Jake can't be registered, either. None of the pups in that litter can be. Remember, that's why Jane Hammond didn't want Delilah to have Sam's pups at first."

Neil still wasn't sure he was convincing Bob. Jane Hammond, their neighbor, had sold three of Jake's litter mates as pet dogs and had kept the fifth to be a working dog on the Hammonds' farm. All the dogs would be happy and cared for, papers or no papers. The only thing their owners couldn't do was show them or use them to breed other pedigree dogs. Neil didn't suppose they wanted to.

"It probably won't make any difference," Bob said. "A dog can't be registered after the age of twelve months, so even if you found out where Sam came from, it's too late to register him now. I don't suppose his original owners bothered to register him before they dumped him by the railroad tracks."

"You never know," Neil said stubbornly. "And it's not too late for Jake."

Bob sighed, got up, and went back to the sink. "You're set on this, aren't you?" he said.

"Yes, I am."

"OK then. We'll all help as much as we can, you know that. Just don't be too disappointed if you don't get anywhere, that's all."

*   *   *

The following morning, a Sunday, Neil helped with the kennel work as he usually did on the weekends, even though his heart wasn't really in it. Once the dogs had been given food and water, he went back into the kitchen and got out the books and Sam's box again, as if going over the records of Sam's achievements could tell him something about his early life.

"Aren't you going to walk Jake?" Emily asked.

Jake leaped to his feet, wagging his tail eagerly, and trotted over to nose Neil's hand. Sam was dozing in his basket and took no notice.

Neil shook his head. "Later, maybe." He opened the scrapbook and started to read the first press article he had pasted in there, about how Sam and Dotty the Dalmatian had caught a purse snatcher at the Compton county show. Sam must have already been ill, but no one would have dreamed it then.

Emily said, "Neil . . ." but Neil didn't answer. He was aware of her standing beside his chair for a minute, and then he heard her sigh and go away. He turned another page of the book.

A little later, the back door opened. He didn't look up, assuming it was his mom, until he heard Chris Wilson's voice saying, "Hi, Neil."

Chris was Neil's best friend at Meadowbank School. He even looked a little like Neil, small and wiry and with the same messy brown hair.

He was standing in the doorway, looking upset. He said, "Emily called and told me about Sam. Neil, I'm really sorry."

Neil's eyes stung and he found himself blinking away tears again. "Nobody's sure. He might be OK," he said tightly.

"I hope so." Chris didn't sound as if he believed it. "He's a great dog. The best." He stood for a minute looking at his feet and then added, "I'm going to bike over to Padsham Castle after lunch and take some photographs for my history project. Do you want to come?"

Normally, Neil would have said yes. But he knew that if he went with Chris everything would feel wrong, because there would be no Sam loping cheerfully along beside the bikes. "No thanks," he mumbled. "I've got things I have to do."

"It won't help to brood about it . . ." Chris began.

Neil stood up and faced him. "It won't help to go off without him, either. You're not going to make me forget about Sam. Just go home, Chris."

Chris looked as if someone had slapped him in the face. "Sorry, Neil."

Neil knew he should apologize, but his throat felt as if he was choking. He sat down again and bent over the scrapbook with his hands on either side of his face to shut out the world.

After a minute, he heard Chris say quietly, "It's OK, Neil. I understand." The kitchen door closed and Neil was by himself again.

He sat turning over the pages of the scrapbook, but now he couldn't read the words of the newspaper reports, or see the pictures. Everything was a blurry haze in front of his eyes.

A chair scraped as someone sat at the table beside him. Emily's voice said, "I was stupid, wasn't I? Calling Chris?"

Thickly, Neil said, "It didn't help."

"I'm sorry." Emily was silent for a minute and then she added, "It's going to be tough at school tomorrow, Neil."

Neil banged the scrapbook shut. "I can deal with it." He pushed his chair back and got to his feet. "Come on, Jake. Walk. You, too, Sam."

He strode across the kitchen with the young Border collie scampering around his feet. Sam roused up as well and padded after them. At the door, Neil turned and looked back at Emily. He could see that she had been crying, too.

"Want to come?" he asked.

Emily managed to smile as she got up from the table. "Course I do."

Emily had been right. School on Monday was tough. Neil could tell that most of his friends had heard the news — probably from Chris. He guessed that Emily had warned them not to talk about Sam, but they all made an effort to be really nice to him, and that was almost worse. Even Hasheem, the class joker, was subdued. Neil was relieved when the bell finally rang for the end of school.

Back at King Street, he met Mike Turner crossing the courtyard at the end of one of his routine inspections of the kennels.

"Are you going to take another look at Sam?" he asked.

"I thought I'd just come and check him over," said Mike, following Neil into the kitchen.

As the vet squatted down beside Sam's basket, Neil said, "Mike, I want to find out about Sam — who his owners were, and why they left him by the railroad tracks. Do you know anything?"

Mike didn't look up from gently feeling for Sam's heartbeat. "Such as what?"

"Well . . . I wondered if anybody had been to see you while their dog was expecting pups. And then never came back when the pups were born. That sort of thing."

Mike thought for a minute and then shook his head. "Nothing comes to mind. It was a long time ago, Neil. If there'd been anything like that, I think I'd have remembered at the time the police brought Sam here. But if it's important to you, I'll get Janice to check the records."

"Thanks," said Neil. "It's very important. If I can find out whether Sam was registered, I might be able to register Jake."

Mike scratched his chin. "There's something I *can* help you with, though," he said thoughtfully. "Did you know that Border collies more than three years old must have an eye test before their pups can be registered?"

"No, I didn't," said Neil.

"Border collies used to have inherited eye conditions, which could mean they would go blind. That's why the eye test was introduced, so breeders wouldn't use dogs who suffered from them. The conditions are very uncommon now."

"Sam would need a test, then." Neil looked down at the Border collie, curled in his basket, looking up at him drowsily as if he would fall asleep at any minute. "Is that a problem?"

"No problem at all," said Mike. "We can do it right now."

He went to his bag, which he had left on the kitchen table, and started to root around in it.

"How do you test a dog's eyesight?" Neil asked.

"Well, he can't read letters off a card," said Mike, "and you can't tell a lot from behavior. Dogs rely on scent much more than they do on sight. What we do is have a look at his eyes and make sure that there isn't any damage."

He turned back from his bag, holding an instrument that looked like a small flashlight with a lens on the top. "This is an ophthalmoscope," he explained. "It lights up the eye so that I can see all of it, front to back."

He squatted down again, took a firm but gentle grip on Sam's head, and switched on the instrument. Neil crouched on Sam's other side, in case the collie was nervous from the light, but Sam didn't try to pull away.

"There's a good boy," Mike said. "Just keep still, and it won't take a minute." To Neil he added, "Sometimes I might use drops to make a dog's pupils widen, but I don't want to mess with Sam any more than necessary."

Neil watched as Mike peered deeply first into one eye and then the other. Finally, he sat back, smiling.

"No problem. His eyes are fine. I'll drop the paper-work off next time I'm out this way."

"What about Jake? Should you test him, too?"

"No, if Sam's fine then he won't have passed it on to Jake. And I know Delilah is in the clear — I tested her for Jane Hammond last year."

"Thanks, Mike," said Neil. Somehow the careful examination and the good result made him feel a lot better. He had made a positive step toward getting Jake registered. "You won't forget about looking in your records, will you?"

The vet was packing his bag again. "No, Neil, I promise. If I come up with anything, I'll give you a call."

He went out. Neil stayed beside the basket, strok-ing Sam gently. "We're going to do it, boy," he said de-terminedly. "We're going to find out just who you are."

CHAPTER FOUR

"Come this way," said Jake Fielding.

It was after school the next day.

Emily had thought of checking the records at the *Compton News* to see if there were any clues to who had left Sam by the railroad tracks. Neil thought it was a great idea.

Jake Fielding was a journalist on the paper — a tall young man with his hair tied back in a ponytail, and his denim jacket and pockets bulging with all the photographic equipment he usually stuffed into them. He had often helped King Street Kennels with publicity for rescue dogs, and he was glad to help now.

Neil and Emily followed him down the hallway at the *Compton News* offices, in the downtown square, and into the room where the archives were kept.

"We're starting to put the old newspapers into the computer," Jake explained, "but the ones you wanted — four years ago, you said? We haven't gone as far back as that yet."

He walked over to a rack on the far wall of the room and pulled out a huge folder made of stiff cardboard. "All the papers are bound in these," he said, laying it on a table and opening it up. "They're a little awkward to handle. Can you manage if I leave you by yourselves?"

"Yes, thanks," said Neil. "We'll be fine."

Jake nodded and went out. Emily had already pulled up a chair and was poring over the folder of newspapers. "These are from June of that year," she said. "When did they bring Sam to King Street?"

Neil thought hard. "It was before that. Sam was the first ever rescue dog, remember, and the rescue center opened in March."

He hoisted the relevant folder out of the rack and opened it up at the other end of the table. Silence fell as they both started to read.

Almost at once, Neil found a big spread about the opening of the King Street Kennels rescue center, with photographs of his mom and dad and the original rescue center building, which was now a dog clinic. "Look at this!" he said to Emily.

Emily came around the table to read it over his shoulder. The article didn't mention Sam. Neil had to read on.

"Here it is!" he said after a few minutes. "It's in the paper for the week after."

Still peering over his shoulder, Emily read the report aloud. *"Police were called out last Tuesday and found a Border collie puppy abandoned by the old railroad tracks. The pup was taken to the new rescue center at King Street Kennels. All efforts to trace his owner have so far failed."*

"That's Sam," said Neil, "but it doesn't tell us anything we didn't know already."

"Try the week after," Emily suggested. "Maybe there'll be something about his owner there."

Neil tried, but though he and Emily worked their way through the papers for the next month, they didn't find any more information. Finally, they had to give up. They were putting the folders back in the rack when Jake Fielding reappeared. "Any luck?" he asked.

"We found the original report," said Neil, "but it didn't tell us anything new."

"Too bad," said Jake.

"Were you working here then?" Emily asked. "Do you remember it?"

Jake shook his head. "Four years ago? No, it was before my time. I was in college."

"There was no name on the story," said Neil. "You can't expect anybody to remember so far back."

"Well, I'll keep my ears open," Jake promised. "I'll let you know if I find out anything."

"Thanks," said Neil.

Jake started to lead the way out of the room and back along the hall. "By the way," he said, "what do you know about this badger killing? I've just been talking to your principal about it."

"We were at the police station when he reported it," Emily replied. "It's just awful."

Jake nodded. "I interviewed Harry Grey at Priorsfield Farm. The den's on his land and he was furious. He's done his best to protect the badgers, but he can't be everywhere at once."

"It's so cruel!" Emily said. "Whoever killed those poor badgers shouldn't get away with it."

"Have you talked to Sergeant Moorhead?" Neil asked. "Did he tell you about the dog who fought with Sam?"

"I have," Jake said, fishing in one pocket of his jacket for a notebook and a pencil. "But he didn't mention a dog."

Neil told him what he knew about the mongrel on the hill, while Jake scribbled notes.

"That's a big help," he said to Neil when he finished. "That's a really good lead."

"Can you put something in the paper?" Emily suggested. "Ask if anyone knows who the dog belongs to? It was really nasty and looked ready to attack anyone. I bet it had something to do with the badgers."

"We might," said Jake. "Remember that we can't prove anything, though."

"We ought to track the dog down," said Emily.

Her indignation was getting the better of her. Neil felt upset about the badgers, too, but he was more interested in tracking down Sam's original owner. He didn't want to waste time talking, especially since he'd just realized where they should go next.

The newspaper story had said the police had been called when Sam was left on the tracks. Maybe the police knew something that didn't appear in the paper. And who had called them? Neil's next stop had to be Sergeant Moorhead, just as soon as he could get Emily to come with him.

*   *   *

When Neil and Emily arrived at the Compton Police Station, Sergeant Moorhead wasn't there, but as they left the station building, the police dog van turned into the courtyard. It stopped and the sergeant got out, followed by Sherlock, his young German shepherd police dog.

Neil remembered all too well when Sergeant Moorhead's previous dog, Jasper, had died bravely in the line of duty. Sergeant Moorhead had found it hard to get over Jasper's death, but he and Sherlock had taken to each other right away, and Neil thought they had the makings of a super team. But he knew that Sergeant Moorhead would never forget Jasper or stop missing him. *Just like me and Sam,* Neil thought.

"Hello," Sergeant Moorhead said when he saw Neil and Emily. "What can I do for you? You haven't heard any more about those badgers, have you?"

"No," said Emily. Neil shook his head.

"I've just been up to the hillside. Somebody phoned and complained about a stray dog in the area — it sounded like that mongrel of yours. But when I got there, it was gone."

"That's where we saw it," Neil said.

"And it's not far from the badger den," Emily added.

"Well," said Sergeant Moorhead, "if the dog was involved, its owner was, too, and we're going to have a tough time proving it. I went to have a look at the den, but there was nothing at all to show who was responsible. Harry Grey didn't see anything."

"But you will find him, won't you?" Emily asked. "If you don't, he'll just go and do it again!"

Sergeant Moorhead took off his police cap and ran a hand over his stubbly gray hair. "I don't know," he admitted. "I've come to a bit of a dead end, and that's a fact."

"But —" Emily began.

Neil interrupted her. He cared more about Sam's background. "Sergeant," he said, "we didn't come about the badgers. We came to ask you about my dog, Sam."

"Sam?" said the sergeant. "What about him?"

Neil began to explain and found that he was telling the sergeant everything, about how Sam had collapsed at the end of the fight and how Mike Turner said that he didn't have long to live. It was the first time he had talked about it, and he only managed to get through the explanation because he could see the understanding in Sergeant Moorhead's eyes.

The sergeant rested a hand on Neil's shoulder for a minute. "That's tough, Neil," he said. "And now you want to find out where Sam came from?" He thought for a minute, and shook his head. "Four years ago? I was with Traffic in the city in those days. I only took charge at Compton when Sergeant Butler retired."

Neil couldn't remember ever meeting Sergeant Butler. "Does he still live around here?" he asked.

"Oh, yes, Ted Butler's still around." Sergeant Moorhead grinned. "He always said he wanted to retire and grow roses, and that's just what he did."

"Would he mind, do you think, if we went to see him?"

"Don't think so." The sergeant locked the door of the dog van and set off toward the police station building with Sherlock trotting obediently at heel. "Come in, and I'll find his address for you."

Neil and Emily followed Sergeant Moorhead inside. He called to someone in the office to look up Sergeant Butler's address, and while they waited he said, "Don't be too disappointed if he doesn't remember. It was a while back."

Neil knew he was right. And Sergeant Butler must have seen a lot of abandoned puppies in his time, before Sam *and* afterward. But this was the only lead he had, and he had to follow it up.

The door from the office opened, and a young constable came out with a sheet of paper in his hand. He gave it to Sergeant Moorhead, who handed it to Neil.

"There you are. Ted Butler's always glad to see visitors. Tell him I sent you."

"We will," Neil said, clutching the paper. "Thanks."

"Just praise his roses," Sergeant Moorhead said with a smile, "and he'll tell you anything you want to know."

*   *   *

When Neil and Emily got back to King Street, Jake came bounding across the courtyard to meet them, jumping up at Neil to welcome him home.

"Down, boy!" Neil said, grinning in spite of his worries. "Don't you know how to behave?"

"You've got your work cut out there," a new voice said.

Neil looked up from Jake to see Glen Paget leaning against the wall near the door of the storeroom. Glen was a student at Padsham Agricultural College, and the boyfriend of Kate McGuire, one of the Parkers' full-time kennel assistants. Neil guessed he was waiting for Kate to finish work. "Hi," he said.

"Hi, Neil. Hi, Emily," said Glen. "Neil, I was really sorry to hear about Sam. If there's anything I can do . . ."

Neil was learning how to cope with people telling him they were sorry, though it still wasn't easy. "Thanks," he said stiffly, "but there's nothing anyone can do."

"Sam's in the yard," Kate said, catching the end of what Neil was saying as she appeared from the storeroom. "He's taking a nap under his special bush. He seemed fairly frisky earlier on, so I took him into the field for a while."

"Thanks." Neil managed to smile at Kate. He knew how upset she had been when she heard about Sam's collapse.

"Glen," Emily said, "have you heard about the dead badgers at Priorsfield Farm?"

"Yes." Glen's face became serious. He hated any kind of cruelty to animals and campaigned for animal rights. "Harry Grey phoned me. He wanted to know if I could warn anyone else with badgers on their land."

"And can you?" Emily asked. "That would be great!"

"Already done," said Glen. "I know several people who are into badger watching. From now on, they'll be watching for the badger killers as well." His face relaxed into a smile, and he wrapped an arm around Emily's shoulders. "Don't you worry. We'll make sure they're stopped."

"We'd better," said Neil. "Before that mongrel does any more damage."

CHAPTER FIVE

Sergeant Butler's house was on the edge of Compton, just off the main Colshaw road. Neil and Emily biked over there after school on Wednesday.

The house stood by itself in the middle of a large garden. Roses scrambled over the wooden fence and a trellis around the porch. More rosebushes flanked the path to the door, and tiny bushes grew in stone containers on either side of the front steps.

"He likes roses, then," said Emily, raising her eyebrows.

"You don't say!"

Neil and Emily propped their bikes against the gatepost and walked up the path. It was a sunny afternoon and the front windows were open, but when Neil pressed the doorbell there was no reply.

"For a retired policeman, he's not very security conscious," said Emily.

"Maybe he had enough of that at work," suggested Neil. "Let's try around the back."

He led the way around the side of the house. There was another garden at the back, a vegetable patch this time, with rows of beans and lettuces. Bees hummed gently back and forth among the scarlet bean flowers.

In the middle of the garden, a man was digging. He was plump, white-haired, and wore old corduroy trousers and a blue shirt with the sleeves rolled up. When he saw Neil and Emily, he drove the spade into the ground and leaned on the handle. "Hello, there. How can I help you?"

"Are you Sergeant Butler?" Neil asked.

"That's me. At least I was. Just Ted Butler now, not Sergeant anymore."

"Sergeant Moorhead sent us," Neil explained. "We'd like to ask you something, if you don't mind."

"I think your roses are gorgeous," said Emily hopefully.

The old man's face broke into a wide smile. "They're not so bad," he said. He pulled out a huge cotton handkerchief and mopped his forehead. "Well, if you want to talk, we'd better go inside."

Neil and Emily followed him up the path into the kitchen. It was an old-fashioned-looking room with a rocking chair pulled up near the kitchen range, and a ginger cat curled up on a rag rug in front of it.

Emily knelt down in front of the cat. "He's lovely! What's his name?"

"Ginger," said Sergeant Butler, washing his hands at the sink, while Neil watched Emily make friends with the cat.

"Well," Sergeant Butler said, turning on a kettle at the back of the range, "what is it you wanted to ask me?"

"It's about my dog, Sam. . . ."

Sergeant Butler sat in the rocking chair, rocking back and forth gently as he listened to Neil. When Neil had finished his explanation, he still went on rocking quietly, his brow furrowed in thought. After a few minutes the kettle started whistling, and he got up to make hot chocolate.

"Border collie puppy, you say? I do remember. We took him up to Bob Parker at King Street Kennels. You'll be Bob's kids, then?"

"That's right," said Neil.

"And you want to know where the puppy came from? I'm not sure I can help you there."

Neil tried to hide his disappointment, while Sergeant Butler took down three cups and saucers from the cupboard. "The newspaper said someone called the police," he said. "Do you know who that was?"

Sergeant Butler shook his head. "Wasn't me that took the call," he said. "I doubt you could find out who did, not now. But I can tell you one thing — the caller didn't give a name."

"They didn't?" Emily exclaimed, sitting upright on the rug.

"No. I always figured it was the pups' owner. For some reason they couldn't keep the little guys, but they didn't want 'em to die out there."

"Nobody traced the call?" Emily asked eagerly.

Sergeant Butler chuckled. "This was the Compton Police, not Scotland Yard."

Neil was sitting open-mouthed as he took in what the sergeant had said. "Just a minute." He got the words out with an effort. "You said 'pups.' 'Them.'"

"That's right." Sergeant Butler started to pour the hot chocolate. "Two of 'em. Both little dogs as alike as two peas."

Neil was still struggling with amazement. "Then what happened to the other one?"

Sergeant Butler gave them both a cup of hot chocolate, and got out a cookie jar. Neil felt almost like screaming with impatience at his slow, careful movements.

"I was up there with the dog van," Sergeant Butler said, "and I found the two little fellows just where the caller said they'd be. Just then this man came past on a bike. He stopped to see what I was doing, and the upshot was, he took one of them with him then and there. And I took the other one up to your dad."

"Sam's got a brother!" said Emily, bright-eyed.

Neil was not so sure that he was pleased to hear the news. For one thing, the Parkers made sure that all their rescue dogs went to suitable owners. They didn't just hand them over to somebody who happened to be passing. "You didn't tell Dad there was another puppy," he said.

"Didn't seem to be any point," said the sergeant. "There was only one left that needed help."

"And what about the man who took the other one?" Emily asked. "Do you know who he was?"

"I'd seen him around," said Sergeant Butler. "He

worked as a signalman on the railroad. Can't say that I remember his name, though."

Neil and Emily tried to think of other questions to ask as they finished their hot chocolate and cookies, but Sergeant Butler couldn't give them any more details. They thanked him and then said good-bye, and he went back to his digging.

As they walked down the path to the gate, Neil said, "That's that, then."

"No, it isn't," said Emily encouragingly. "What about the signalman?"

"He won't know anything." Neil felt a black cloud of disappointment settling over him. "He didn't see the puppies until after they were abandoned."

"It's worth a try, though," Emily insisted. "Anyway, don't you want to see Sam's brother?"

"Maybe," said Neil. Inside, he thought, *A healthy dog, when Sam's dying? I don't know.*

"We could find out," Emily went on. "Sergeant Butler didn't know his name, but they must know at the station. A signalman with a Border collie. We could ask."

"OK." Neil still wasn't sure he wanted to go on with this, but he knew he would never forgive himself if he gave up the last chance of finding out the truth about Sam. "I'll tell you one thing," he added as he mounted his bike and turned toward home, "the police station is a lot more efficient now that Sergeant Moorhead's in charge."

*   *   *

Neil and Emily decided not to visit the station until the weekend. Neil felt he had already spent a lot of time on the investigation that he ought to have spent with Sam. In the old days, of course, Sam would have come with him. Neil found it hard to believe that would never happen again.

The only new information Neil found out was when Mike Turner phoned on Thursday to say that his nurse Janice had checked the practice records from around the time the pups were abandoned. There were no pregnant Border collies or Border collie puppies except ones that Mike could identify. Another of Neil's leads had fizzled out.

That night after school, he tried to put the whole thing out of his mind by updating the King Street Kennels web site on the office computer. There was a picture of the newest rescue dog, a borzoi, to be scanned in, and a couple of other pictures to be deleted because the dogs had already gone to new homes.

Carole came in while he was working and started to stick stamps on the letters in her out-tray. "That's great, Neil," she said. "I haven't had time to do anything with it this week. It's taking me all my time to get ready for Emily's birthday."

Neil felt a pang of guilt. In the last few days, while he was searching for information about Sam, he hadn't thought about Emily's birthday once. And Emily had given up so much of her time to help him.

With the birthday and the party a week from Saturday, Neil realized that there wasn't long to go. "I haven't bought her a present yet," he said.

Carole looked up from the envelopes. "Are you all right for money?"

"Sure. I just don't know what to get her."

"Anything to do with animals," Carole said, smiling. "Why don't you try Warren's on Main Street? They've got lots of nice stuff."

"I might," Neil said. He would like to give Emily something really special, but he couldn't think what. "What are you and Dad getting her?" he asked.

Carole paused as she was about to lick a stamp. "Can't say," she said. "It's a secret." Carole grinned. "I know you and Emily. You're as thick as thieves. If I tell you what her big present is going to be, you'll give it away to her. Maybe without even meaning to."

"I won't, Mom, honest."

"Well . . ." Carole stamped the last of the letters and bundled them up ready for the post office. She had a mischievous glint in her eye. "All right, then, I'll tell you. But it's a big secret, OK? We're giving her a leopard."

For a few seconds, Neil believed her. He opened his mouth to say, "No way! It'll eat the dogs!" Then he realized, and let out a long, elaborate sigh instead. "Oh, very funny, Mom."

"No, really." Carole was trying hard to stay straight-faced. "A leopard. Don't you think she'll like it?"

Neil was ready to bet that Emily would like it very much. He could just see her grooming it and taking it for walks. "OK," he said. "If you won't tell me, you won't. But don't expect me to believe that!"

Carole shrugged. "Suit yourself. Do you want to take these down to the mailbox? You could take Sam — it's not far, and the walk would be good for him."

"Yes, sure." Neil gave up the idea of getting his mom to say any more. "Just as soon as I've finished the web site."

When he had logged off and switched off the computer, he went into the kitchen to get Sam. Emily was sitting at the table writing out invitation cards to her party, while Sarah cut out paper doilies and place mats. Jake was sniffing at the scraps of paper she let fall to the floor.

Bob was standing over the stove, stirring something in a huge pan. "You're not going out now, Neil?" he asked. "Dinner's almost ready."

"Just down to the mailbox for Mom," Neil explained. "She thought it would be a good walk for Sam."

At the sound of his name, Sam got up from his basket with something of his old alertness. "Come on, boy," Neil said, his heart aching. When his dog looked like that, he couldn't help hoping that Mike was wrong and that Sam was getting better.

"All right," Bob said, "but don't be long. Dinner in

ten minutes. I'll want that table cleared," he added to Emily and Sarah.

"Almost done," said Emily.

"It's going to be a great party," Sarah said, smiling widely. "I bet you'll like my present best. But I'm not going to tell you what it is. It's a secret."

"That's all right," Emily said. "I love secrets."

As he went out with Sam and Jake, who had insisted on coming, too, Neil couldn't help feeling depressed. Everybody seemed to have good surprises saved up for Emily. Except for him. He wanted to join in the fun, but with Sam's illness hanging over him, he couldn't make himself care.

"It'll be OK," he muttered to himself. "I won't spoil it. But I know what I'd ask for if it was my birthday."

He reached a hand down and patted Sam. Sam's life was a present that nobody could give him. But second best — a long way second but still important — was to find out about Sam's pedigree.

"That signalman might know something," he said aloud as he walked down the drive with the dogs at heel. Without meaning to, he had pushed Emily's birthday to the back of his mind again. "He's got to!"

CHAPTER SIX

On Saturday morning, Neil started his day by helping with the kennel work. There was more to do than usual because Bev, the new full-time kennel assistant at King Street, had gone off to Cornwall for a short break with her dog, Milly.

Kate McGuire was getting some of the boarding pens ready for new arrivals who were expected later in the day, and Neil went to the storeroom for baskets and bedding. He couldn't help noticing, neatly stacked in one corner, some of the boxes and planks that he had used to set up Agility courses for Sam's training in the exercise field. Sam hadn't needed them for a long time now. He would never need them again.

Neil swallowed a lump in his throat. He was being stupid, he told himself fiercely, to get worked up about a few old boxes. *I'll get them out and start Jake's training,* he thought. *Soon. But not right now.*

When the pens were spick-and-span, Kate and Emily got some of the bigger dogs ready for a walk.

"Em, will you take Jake?" Neil asked. "I want to spend some time with Sam."

"Sure," Emily said. She laughed and rumpled Jake's ears as he bounced up to her. "Come on, trouble. See if you can find some rabbits on the hillside."

"I thought we weren't supposed to go up there," Neil said. "Because of that mongrel."

"We'll go the other way," Kate said, coming up with two of the boarding dogs on their leashes. "And we won't let the dogs run free."

"It's not fair!" said Emily. "The hill path should be for everybody, and now it's spoiled."

"The sooner they catch that dog the better," said Neil.

He watched Kate and Emily and the dogs as they crossed the exercise field, and then whistled to Sam, who was snoozing in his favorite spot under the bushes at the end of the garden. As he came padding up, Neil crouched down and hugged him. Sam looked up at him trustfully.

"You're the best, Sam," Neil said quietly. "You always will be."

Compton Station on Saturday was a busy place. When Neil and Emily arrived with Jake late in the morning, it looked as if half of Compton had decided to take the train into Manchester to go shopping.

Carole had dropped them on her way into town, and the weather was hotter than ever.

There was a line at the ticket office, but only one elderly man waiting at the information window. When he had gone, Neil went up to the woman on duty. "Excuse me . . ."

"Yes, dear?" the woman said. "Where do you want to go?"

"I don't want to go anywhere. I'm trying to find somebody who works here."

"Find somebody? Find who?"

"I'm not sure." Neil could see that the woman was

starting to look annoyed, as if she thought he was wasting her time. Somebody else had joined the line behind him. "He's a signalman," he said.

"We've got a lot of signalmen."

"And he's got a dog like mine."

The woman peered over the edge of the information window so that she could see Jake. Jake put his paws up against the wall and gave her a doggy grin, his tongue lolling as he panted vigorously. The woman smiled. "Oh, you should've said! That'll be Jim Brewster."

"Is he here, please?" Emily asked.

"He's around somewhere," the woman said, "because that's his bike, over there in the rack." She pointed to a scruffy old bicycle at the very end. "But he'll be down the line. You can't talk to him now."

Neil could hear the person in the line behind him fidgeting impatiently. "When does he stop work, then?"

"Six o'clock," the woman said promptly. "Now, if you don't mind, I've got people to see to. Next, please!"

Neil moved away from the window, ignoring the glare from the woman in line behind him.

"We'll have to come back," Emily said.

"Six o'clock!" Neil said disgustedly, scuffing his feet. "We won't get anything else done today if we can't talk to him before six o'clock."

Emily shrugged. "Well, we —" She broke off, and grabbed at Neil's arm. "Neil! Look!"

A man in overalls had just come out of the station.

A beautiful black-and-white Border collie was trotting at his heels.

Neil caught his breath.

The dog looked exactly like Sam!

The man was whistling cheerfully as he went over to the scruffy bike and took a sandwich box out of the saddlebag.

Neil exchanged a glance with Emily and walked over to him. "Excuse me, are you Jim Brewster?"

The man turned around. He was short and plump, with brown hair turning gray and a lined, sunburned face. "That's me," he said.

"I'm Neil Parker," said Neil. "And this is my sister, Emily. We're from King Street Kennels. Can I ask you something, please? It's about your dog."

Mr. Brewster looked puzzled but answered Neil's question cheerfully. "I don't see why you'd want to know about my Skip. But ask away."

Neil bent down and held out his hand for Skip to sniff, and then rumpled his ears and gave him one of the dog treats he always carried in his pockets. Jake came up and pushed his muzzle into Neil's hand, looking for a treat of his own.

Skip was bright-eyed and lively, and looked ready to be friends. *Just how Sam used to be,* Neil thought sadly. With an effort, he made himself concentrate on what he had come to find out. "You got him when he was abandoned on the branch line, didn't you?"

"Yes, that's right."

"Do you remember the other puppy?" When Jim Brewster nodded, Neil went on more excitedly, "Well, he's my dog now. His name is Sam."

Jim Brewster looked at Jake, and shook his head. "No, lad, that dog's too young."

"No, this is Jake," Neil explained. "Sam's son."

"Sergeant Butler brought Sam to the rescue center at King Street," Emily added. "That's how Neil got him."

Jim hitched himself onto the low wall of the station courtyard and snapped his fingers at Skip, who trotted up and sat at his feet. Neil couldn't get over how much like Sam the other Border collie looked. If you had put them side by side, it would have been hard to tell them apart.

"I think Sam has a little more white on his front," he said.

Jim nodded. "And this young one is his son?" he said. He held his hand out to Jake. "Come on, fella. Come and say hello to your Uncle Skip."

While the two dogs cautiously sniffed each other, Jim went on, "Well, you haven't come to find me just to say hello. What can I do for you?"

"I'm trying to find out more about Sam," Neil explained. He didn't feel that he wanted to go into all the reasons or tell Jim Brewster that Sam was dying. Seeing Skip, so obviously healthy and cared for, was enough without that. "Sergeant Butler told us that you came along when he found the pups on the

old branch line. I wondered whether you saw anything that might help me find out who their owners
were."

Jim shook his head. "Whoever it was, they won't
want to be found. Not when they'd do that to a couple of little puppies. Now . . ." He scratched his gray-
ing hair. "I was biking along the path up there when
I saw the police dog van. The pups were partway up
the embankment. I'll tell you one thing."

"What's that?" Neil asked eagerly.

"There's no road near there. Sergeant Butler had his
work cut out getting the dog van up the track. Whoever dumped the puppies there must have walked or
come on a bike."

"That might mean they hadn't come far!" Emily said.

"That's what I figure," said Jim. "It's a long time ago, but you might start by asking around at the nearest houses — that would be the Railway Cottages."

Emily and Neil exchanged a puzzled look. "I don't know where they are," said Neil.

"There's an abandoned station up there," Jim explained. "At the end of the branch line. The Railway Cottages lead up to it, off Padsham Road. It's where the railroad workers used to live, when the line was still in use."

"I think I know," said Emily. "It's not far away from Priorsfield Farm."

"That's right," said Jim.

"So what are we waiting for?" said Neil. "Let's go. Thanks for everything, Mr. Brewster."

"I haven't done much."

"I'll bring Sam to see you, just as soon as I can," Neil promised. He couldn't think of any better way to show Jim Brewster how grateful he was for this new information. He bent down to give Skip a last pat. "You'd like to see your brother, wouldn't you, Skip?"

After their visit to the station, Neil and Emily had to go home for lunch, so it was the middle of the afternoon before they continued their search. Neil had left Jake at home this time. The young dog was tired after his energetic morning, and he had settled down for a snooze in the yard with Sam.

"This must be it," said Neil. He brought his bike to a halt and put one foot to the ground. A narrow road led off to the left. The hedges on either side were overgrown, and brambles almost covered the sign that said RAILWAY COTTAGES.

"At least it looks cooler down there," said Emily, wiping her forehead on her sleeve.

Because the road was very narrow and winding, they pushed the bikes and walked in single file. Behind the hedge to the left were fields; Neil thought they must be part of Priorsfield Farm, though they were nowhere near the farmhouse. As they walked down the winding road, Neil hoped Emily wouldn't start getting worked up about the badgers again. Not that he didn't care, but he had other things on his mind.

On the other side of the road, the hedge gave way to a terrace of gray cottages, each with a small square yard in front of it. Neil and Emily propped their bikes by the first one.

"Now what?" said Emily.

"Let's walk down to the end first," said Neil. "We might see something."

They walked along the terrace, carefully examining each of the houses as they passed it. Neil had been half hoping to see a Border collie who might have been Sam's mom, but there wasn't any sign of dogs.

At the end of the terrace was a space that had been graveled, though now weeds were growing over it. Beyond it was the abandoned station, silent and boarded up, and a phone booth.

"OK," said Neil. "We'll start asking at the houses."

At the house nearest the station, the yard was paved over except for a small circular pond in the middle where there was a statue of a gnome fishing. Neil lifted the brass knocker on the door and brought it down sharply. After a minute the door opened an inch or two, and a hatchet-faced woman poked her head out. "Yes?"

"Excuse me," said Neil politely, "I'd like to ask if you have a dog."

"A dog? Nasty filthy creatures! You won't see any dogs around here!" She slammed the door.

"Well!" said Emily.

"*She'd* abandon puppies," Neil muttered as he turned away.

"Yes, but she wouldn't *have* them in the first place," Emily pointed out.

There was no reply at the next two houses, and the one after that looked empty, with a real estate agent's board sagging at the gate.

There was a tricycle and a small plastic wheelbarrow in the next yard, and as Neil approached the front door he could hear a baby screaming.

"Dogs?" the woman asked when she opened the door; another small child was clinging around her legs. "Three children, two hamsters, and a cat are more than enough for me!" She smiled. The baby was still crying in the background. "Sorry, I've got to go."

Neil was starting to feel depressed.

At the next house, Neil knocked twice and was about to leave when he heard the faint shuffling of feet from the other side of the door. He waited, then the door opened a crack, held by a chain. An old woman with wispy white hair peered out at him.

"Excuse me," Neil said again. "Would you mind telling me if you have a dog?"

The old woman blinked nervously at him. "A dog, dear? No, I don't have a dog."

"Have you ever had one?"

The woman glanced sharply from Neil to Emily and back again. "What is this? Why do you want to know? I can't tell you anything."

"It's just that we . . ." Emily began, but the old woman was already swinging the door shut. Neil heard the chain rattling.

"Uh-oh," he said.

"I think we scared her," said Emily sympathetically. "We should have explained who we are."

Along the rest of the terrace were more houses with no reply, one woman who thought they were from the gas company, and a man who was furious because they woke him up from his sleep after the night shift. The only dog owner — the gas company woman — had a Yorkshire terrier.

Discouraged, Neil and Emily went back to their bikes.

"That's that," said Neil. "And I don't know where to look next."

"What about down there?" Emily pointed to a narrow lane that led off from the other side of the road.

"That probably just goes to Priorsfield Farm."

"Well, we don't know if it does," Emily insisted. "We might as well check it out."

Neil shrugged. "OK."

The lane was deeply rutted, just wide enough for a single car. Neil thought it must be a back entrance to Priorsfield, but after about a hundred yards they reached a rusty five-barred gate leading to a cobbled yard with a house and farm buildings beyond it.

The paint on the house was peeling and the windows looked dirty, but someone obviously lived there. A blue van was parked beside the door, and a few hens were pecking here and there. Neil could hear a dog barking.

"What a dump!" Emily said.

"We'd better try," Neil said. "We're not giving up now."

He reached out for the loop of ratty string that kept the gate closed, and at that moment the dog started to bark more furiously and raced out of the half-open barn door.

Neil pushed the string back into place and took a step back, staring. In front of him, standing stiff-legged and barking fit to burst, was the rusty-coated mongrel that had attacked Jake and Sam on the hillside.

CHAPTER SEVEN

The dog kept barking. For a few seconds, Neil and Emily were both frozen with shock. Then Emily seized the string on the gatepost again.

"I'm going in. I'm going to tell the farmer just what his dog has been doing!"

"Oh, no, you're not." Neil stood in front of her so she couldn't open the gate. "Get real, Em. If you set foot in there, that dog will go for you. Besides, his owner doesn't care, or he wouldn't let him wander like that."

Emily stood her ground for a minute, her eyes fixed rebelliously on her brother's face. Then she took a step back. "What, then?"

"There's a phone booth by the abandoned station. We'll call Sergeant Moorhead."

"All right."

They retraced their steps along the track and back to the pay phone. To Neil's relief, it still worked. He fished in his pockets until he found change so that he could call the police station direct.

When he asked for Sergeant Moorhead the voice at the other end told him to hold on, and after a couple of minutes the sergeant came on the line. "Yes? What is it?"

"This is Neil Parker. I've found that mongrel."

"What? Where?"

Neil gave the sergeant directions.

"I'm on my way," said Sergeant Moorhead. "You stay by the phone booth until I come. And stay out of trouble!"

Neil and Emily didn't have to wait long until the sergeant appeared at the wheel of the police dog van, with Sherlock sitting behind him. Sergeant Moorhead pulled up at the end of the lane that led to the farm. "OK, hop in," he said, when Neil and Emily came rushing up to him. "I'll need you to identify the dog, but let me do the talking." He looked at Neil and raised his eyebrows. Neil thought it would be best to keep quiet.

Sergeant Moorhead drove down the road and pulled up outside the gates of the farm. The farmyard was empty again, apart from the hens, but as Neil and Emily piled out of the van behind the sergeant and Sherlock, a man appeared from the barn with the mongrel at his heels. He was tall with brown hair, muddy checked trousers, and a corduroy shirt.

He strode across the farmyard to the gate. The mongrel followed and bared its teeth at Sherlock through the bars.

"Afternoon, Sergeant," said the farmer.

"Could I have your name, sir?"

"Jack Wragg. What can I do for you?"

"I've had a complaint about your dog, sir," said Sergeant Moorhead. "He's been wandering on the hillside, and I've had a report that suggests he might be dangerous."

"He attacked my dog," said Neil, "and he would have attacked me!"

The farmer shrugged.

Sergeant Moorhead turned to Neil. "You're sure this is the same dog?"

"Positive."

"I think, Mr. Wragg, I'm going to have to take the dog," Sergeant Moorhead went on. "The court will decide whether to make an order for him to be kept under proper control, or whether he's so dangerous that he'll have to be destroyed."

Jack Wragg stared at the sergeant. Neil thought he looked angry, but not nearly as upset as he should have at the thought of losing his dog.

"Are you telling me I can't let my own dog out for a run if I want to?" he asked aggressively.

"Not if he attacks children, Mr. Wragg."

"I don't know anything about him attacking children," the farmer said.

"And kills badgers!" Emily added.

Neil stifled a groan. He knew how bad Emily felt about the wrecked badger home — he felt bad himself — but that wasn't the right way to bring it up. If Jack Wragg denied it, how were they going to prove anything?

Sergeant Moorhead gave Emily an exasperated look. "Mr. Wragg, do you know anything about the damage to the badger den at Priorsfield Farm?"

"Yes. It was me and Grip here." The farmer looked really angry. "Why not? Badgers are vermin. They give diseases to cows."

Neil was astonished that Jack Wragg was prepared to admit what he'd done. He didn't even seem to think it was wrong.

"That's not true!" said Emily hotly.

"Well, that's certainly no excuse for taking the law into your own hands," said Sergeant Moorhead. "You've broken the law by killing the badgers, and you'll have to answer to charges of trespassing on Harry Grey's land."

Jack Wragg made a disgusted noise. "My cows are my living," he said. "I won't have them threatened by badgers, or by stupid sentimental people who don't understand the countryside." He looked at Emily with a fierce scowl.

"The law's the law, Mr. Wragg," said the sergeant. "I'm afraid you'll have to come with me to the police station and make a statement."

Sergeant Moorhead read Jack Wragg his rights. For a moment, Neil thought the farmer would resist, or even set his dog on the sergeant. But he shrugged. "Got no choice, have I? Come on, Grip."

As Jack Wragg swung the gate open, Neil had a new idea. "Mr. Wragg, have you ever had a Border collie?"

The farmer stared at him. "What's it to you?"

"I'm looking for someone around here with a pedigreed Border collie — or somebody who once had one."

"Well, I haven't," Mr. Wragg sneered. "Do you think I could afford a fancy dog like that?"

Neil looked around at the farm and realized that times were obviously really hard for the farmer.

The man went toward the house and shouted inside that he was going out and wouldn't be long. Neil had mixed feelings as he watched the sergeant help the man put his dog in a large cage in the back of the dog van. Jack Wragg gave Grip a gentle pat as the dog settled into his cage, then climbed into the front seat next to Sergeant Moorhead.

The sergeant leaned out of the window as he started the engine. "Thanks, Neil, Emily. You've done a good job. I'll be in touch — you'll probably have to give a statement."

He drove away down the lane. Neil and Emily followed on foot, back to where they had left the bikes.

"He was horrible," said Emily. "I hope they put him in prison for years and years and years!"

"I don't," said Neil. He couldn't help a sense of triumph, but in spite of what Grip had done to Sam, in spite of the dead badgers, he was surprised to find himself a little bit sorry for Jack Wragg and the mongrel. "He thought he was protecting his cows. I know he shouldn't have let his dog be so aggressive, but . . . well, I know what it's like to think you're going to lose your dog."

*   *   *

Neil felt satisfied that they had solved the mystery of the mongrel, and the hillside was safe to walk on again. At school the following week, Mr. Hamley told the story in assembly hall, and it seemed to Neil as if every kid in the place came up to congratulate him and Emily.

When he arrived home on Tuesday he found a message from Sergeant Moorhead, saying that Jack Wragg had been charged with trespassing and killing the badgers and with keeping a dangerous dog. Neil and Emily would be needed as witnesses when the case came up.

The only mystery Neil couldn't solve was the one about Sam's background. He couldn't think of anyone else to ask or anywhere to go to find out more than he knew already. The trail seemed to have gone cold.

After school on Thursday, Neil decided it was time to pull himself together. He had to stop brooding about Sam. After all, his dog was still alive, and the first panic after the fight on the hillside was over.

He began to hope again.

And he realized that there wasn't much time left to get ready for Emily's birthday. He'd told his mom and dad that he would go into Compton by himself after school to buy Emily's present. He was getting his bike out of the shed when Chris Wilson came in. "Hi, Neil," he said.

Since Chris's disastrous visit to King Street, he and Neil hadn't really been on their old friendly terms. Neil had been too wrapped up in Sam, and, for more than a week, Chris hadn't asked him to soccer practice or if he wanted to go on a bike ride. Now Neil felt embarrassed as he said hi. He'd been rotten to Chris, and none of it had been his friend's fault.

"That was great about the badgers," said Chris.

"We were just lucky," said Neil. He wanted to be friends with Chris again, but he wasn't quite sure what to say. He got his bike out and fiddled with the pedals. Then he looked up. "Chris, I'm sorry —"

At the same time Chris said, "Neil, I'm really sorry —"

They both burst out laughing. Chris gave Neil a friendly punch on the shoulder.

Neil said, "Chris, it's Em's birthday on Saturday. Why don't you come to her party? Mom always lets me invite somebody."

Chris gave him a wide grin. "Sure, Neil. I'd like that."

"Great. Two o'clock, OK? I'll see you there."

When Chris had gone, Neil pedaled into Compton town center. The weather had turned overcast and thundering, and Neil felt his T-shirt sticking to him. There was going to be a storm.

He still didn't know what to buy for Emily but, as

his mom had suggested, he decided to try Warren's on Main Street. It was a gift shop — everything they sold was eco-friendly and nothing was tested on animals. Neil knew that was right up Emily's alley.

He left his bike outside the shop and went in. The shelves were full of attractive things: stationery, mugs, patterned boxes, pictures, and fancy frames. Neil considered some jewelry with animals painted on it, but Emily wasn't really a jewelry person.

"Can I help you?"

He turned around to see the shop assistant standing beside him. She was a tall young woman about Kate McGuire's age, with short blond curls. She wore a stylish blue dress and a badge with her name on it: ANNE.

"I'm looking for a birthday present for my sister," Neil said. "She'll be ten on Saturday."

"What kind of things does she like?" Anne asked.

"Animals! She's crazy about animals."

"Well, have you thought about writing paper?" Anne suggested. "Or what about these picture frames?"

She showed him a pottery frame decorated with a dog's head in one corner — a black-and-white Border collie.

"That's just like my dog," Neil said.

"Not your sister's? Well, then . . ."

"Emily doesn't have a pet," Neil said. *Unless Mom and Dad give her that leopard.* In case Anne thought

Emily was missing out, he added quickly, "We live at King Street Kennels. She looks after all the dogs."

"A different kind of dog, then," Anne said, looking around the shop. "I like Border collies best, though."

"So do I! Do you have one of your own?"

"No, I've only got a tiny apartment, and I'm out all day. It wouldn't be fair to the dog. When I was at school, though, I used to walk a Border collie for an old lady. She was lovely — the dog, I mean. Her name was Betsy."

Neil was only half listening. The rest of his attention was on wondering what to buy for Emily.

Then he froze as Anne said, "Betsy was going to have puppies. I was really upset when she died."

For a second Neil couldn't find enough breath to ask his next question. It came out too loud. "What happened to the puppies?"

"They died, too, I think."

"Where did the old lady live?" Neil asked. He was too eager to lead up to the information gradually.

Anne gave him a sharp look. "Why do you want to know?"

"Oh — Dad might know her," Neil said hastily. "He knows almost everyone in Compton with a dog."

"Oh, well . . ." Anne shrugged, as if it didn't really matter to her. "Her name was Mrs. Atkinson. She lived in the Railway Cottages . . . I can't remember the number. I lost touch with her after her dog died."

Just then, the shop bell rang as another customer

came in. While Anne waited on him, Neil managed to pull himself together. The timing must be about right, if Anne had still been in school but old enough to be trusted with someone's dog. The place was right, and if the mother dog had died — maybe when her puppies were born — that could explain why the pups had been abandoned.

"It's time I had a talk with Mrs. Atkinson of the Railway Cottages," Neil muttered to himself.

He forced himself to think about Emily's present again, and finally chose a mobile for her, with wind chimes hanging from a carved wooden dog. Anne gift-wrapped it for him.

"I hope your sister has a happy birthday," she said as Neil left the shop.

"Thanks, I'll tell her." *It might just be a good day for everybody*, he thought, getting on his bike and heading home.

CHAPTER EIGHT

Neil's instincts told him to head for the Railway Cottages right away. But he made himself go home instead. Emily had helped him right from the start of the search; it was only fair that she should be in at the end of it. Besides, he knew it would be better if he thought about what he was going to say before he spoke to Mrs. Atkinson.

By the time Neil had told Emily what he had found out and helped his mom and dad with the kennel work, it was too late to go out to the Railway Cottages that day. They had to wait until school was over on Friday.

"I want to take Sam," Neil said, as he and Emily got ready to leave.

Mike Turner had told him that Sam's heart might

have been damaged by the stress of being abandoned on the railroad tracks. Neil wanted to show Mrs. Atkinson what she had done.

"Won't it be too far for him?" Emily asked. "And he can't keep up with the bikes."

Sam looked up at them both eagerly.

"We won't go on the bikes. If we walk along the hillside, it's not so far. It's OK to go there now that that mongrel isn't on the loose. And Mike said to treat him normally."

He got Sam's leash and clipped it on. Jake was bouncing around excitedly, whining and pawing at Neil's legs. "OK, you, too," Neil said. "But try not to excite Sam."

They set off, telling Bob and Carole that they were taking the dogs for a walk. Neil hadn't told his mom and dad what he was really doing. He was afraid they might stop him or want to go with him, and this was something Neil felt he had to do himself.

The weather was hot and even stickier than the day before. Thunder clouds were building up over the hill. Emily paused, looking up. "There's going to be a storm. I hope we don't get caught in it."

Neil was too worked up to start worrying about the weather. "Let's get going, then."

Instead of climbing the hill, they followed a path along its foot that eventually led to the edge of Priorsfield Farm and along the river. For a few hundred yards, the river joined the old branch line, and then veered away. Neil and Emily crossed a rickety wooden bridge and went on following the tracks until they came to the abandoned station. Neil realized they must have passed the place where Sam and Skip had been found, but he wasn't sure exactly where that was.

The sky was even darker as they reached the road. A hot breeze was blowing back the leaves on the trees, and thunder mumbled in the distance. A few drops of rain spattered in the dust.

"Any minute now," said Emily.

Before he left home, Neil had looked up Mrs. Atkinson in the phone book and found that she lived at number 15.

"Isn't that the old lady we spoke to?" asked Emily. "The one who looked so scared?"

"Maybe she looked scared because she felt guilty," said Neil. "If she is the one, she's got plenty to be guilty about."

Now, as they walked down to the Railway Cottages, he realized Emily was right. He went up to number 15 and knocked. Sam sat beside him on the step while Emily came up behind with Jake.

Again there was the wait while slow footsteps came to the door. It opened a few inches and the white-haired old woman looked out nervously.

"Mrs. Atkinson," said Neil, "do you recognize this dog?"

The woman looked down at Sam. To Neil's horror

and astonishment, tears welled up in her eyes. "He looks just like my Betsy." She started to close the door. Neil thought she was going to shut them out, but then she took the chain off and held the door wide open. "You'd better come in," said Mrs. Atkinson.

A few minutes later, Neil was sitting on a prickly old sofa with the dogs at his feet. Emily was comforting Mrs. Atkinson, who had started to cry after she'd showed them in.

"I'm Emily Parker from King Street Kennels," she explained. "And this is my brother, Neil. We've been trying to find out about Neil's dogs."

The room was packed with furniture and was dark from the clouds that were gathering outside. Every surface was covered with ornaments and photographs, and everything could have used a good dusting. In the middle of the mantelpiece was a photograph that Neil could see was special, bigger than the others, in a silver frame. It showed a beautiful Border collie, with shining eyes and a glossy coat.

"That's my Betsy," Mrs. Atkinson said, dabbing her eyes with a handkerchief. "She was the gentlest, most beautiful dog you could wish for."

"Can you tell us about her?" Emily said, with a fierce look at Neil that clearly told him to be quiet. Emily needn't have worried. Far from being angry, Neil was just bewildered. He had built up in his

mind the picture of Sam's first owner as being wicked. He wasn't prepared for this helpless old lady who couldn't think about her dog without crying.

"She was always a healthy dog," Mrs. Atkinson began, "and she seemed fine when she was expecting the puppies. It wasn't her first litter. I delivered them myself, because I couldn't really afford to call the vet. And there didn't seem to be any complications. There were three of them — two little boys and a girl."

"Three!" Neil exclaimed.

"What happened then?" Emily asked, giving Neil another warning look.

Mrs. Atkinson twisted her hands together. "Betsy died. It was terrible! I still don't know why it happened. The puppies were about three weeks old, and everything had been fine until then."

"So what went wrong?" asked Neil.

"I don't know! One minute Betsy was feeding the puppies, looking really happy and contented, and then she started shivering and twitching. I thought she might be cold, and I started the fire up, but then she got up and started staggering around. She looked so frightened, and I didn't know what to do for her." Mrs. Atkinson's mouth started to tremble and her voice sounded choked as she went on. "Then she collapsed, jerking as if she was having a seizure. I went over to her and tried to hold her, but she . . . she just died."

"Milk fever," Neil said as the old lady finished her story. "Mike Turner told me that mother dogs can often get it while they're feeding their puppies. It's because they're short of calcium. You should have called the vet," he told Mrs. Atkinson. "If your dog had been given an injection in time, she might not have died."

"Neil!" said Emily, as Mrs. Atkinson burst into tears again.

"Oh, I know, I know . . ." the old lady said. "But I couldn't afford it, and it all happened so quickly. By the time I realized I would have to call him and worry about the expense later, Betsy was dead."

Emily gave her time to control herself again and then asked gently, "And what happened after that?"

"I tried to feed the puppies myself. But they wouldn't feed properly from a bottle, and then the little girl died, too. The others were getting weaker and I knew I had to do something, so I carried them up onto the railroad tracks and then phoned the police to come and get them. I didn't know what else to do."

"Why didn't you call the SPCA?" Neil asked.

Mrs. Atkinson looked ashamed. "I was afraid of getting into trouble. I'd made such a mess of everything by then — two dogs dead — and I thought they would take me to court if they knew what I'd done."

Emily reached out and patted her hand. Neil, too, was starting to feel sorry for her, but he still couldn't believe that leaving two weak little puppies on the branch line was the best she could have done. He said, "If you'd brought them to Dad's rescue center, he would have helped you."

"I didn't know about the rescue center — not then," Mrs. Atkinson explained. "If I had . . . things might have been different."

"It had only just opened," admitted Neil. Suddenly, he found that he could smile at Mrs. Atkinson. "Would you like to know what happened to those two puppies?"

All the time they had been talking, Mrs. Atkinson

had been darting glances at Sam and Jake. "Yes, please," she said.

"Well," said Neil, beginning to relax. "One is a dog called Skip, who belongs to a signalman at Compton Station. He's a great dog. And the other one . . ." He reached down to rest his hand on Sam's head. "Is Sam here."

"Oh!" A watery smile appeared on Mrs. Atkinson's face. "Is he really? Would he let me pet him, do you think?"

"Sure," said Neil. He fished out a handful of dog treats from his pocket and handed them to her. "Give him one or two of those."

Mrs. Atkinson held out one of the treats to Sam, who snuffled it up and sat quietly beside her while she stroked his head. Jake came nosing up, demanding his share, resting a paw on Mrs. Atkinson's knee. She was smiling as if she couldn't believe they were really there.

"And this," Neil went on, pointing at Jake and pausing for effect, "is Sam's son."

"Oh . . ." Mrs. Atkinson's hand was shaking as she held out the treat for Jake. "Betsy's grandson! He's lovely!"

Neil *had* intended to tell her all about Sam's illness, and how Mike Turner thought his heart might have been damaged because he had been abandoned at such an early age. He had meant to accuse her.

Now he found he couldn't do it.

The dogs have forgiven her, Neil thought. Perhaps he could forgive her as well.

Thunder crashed and rolled overhead, and Neil realized that it had been raining hard for some time. He had been so eager to hear the story about the puppies that he had not noticed the exact moment when the storm started for real.

Meanwhile, Emily had found her way into the kitchen. Neil heard her putting on the kettle, and the rattle of teacups. A few minutes later she came back with a tray of tea.

"Thank you, dear," said Mrs. Atkinson. "Will you pour? I still feel all shaky. Do you know, I've never gotten over it, after all this time."

"Tell me, Mrs. Atkinson," Neil said, when they were all drinking tea, "was Betsy a pedigreed dog?"

"My Betsy?" Mrs. Atkinson's eyes shone with pride. "Of course she was! She had champions in her line."

Neil felt a smile begin to appear on his face.

Emily nudged him and grinned.

Neil had always known Sam had a good pedigree, but it felt fantastic to be proved right. "And the puppies' father?" he went on eagerly.

Mrs. Atkinson nodded.

"I don't suppose . . ." Neil could hardly get the question out — the answer was so important. "I don't suppose you registered the puppies, did you?"

"Yes, I did. I was hoping to sell them, you see. They were very good puppies — or they would have been."

"And what happened to the documents?"

Mrs. Atkinson frowned. "I'm not sure I remember . . . I sent the forms off as soon as the puppies were born, but by the time the documents came back, Betsy was dead, and the little female puppy, and I'd gotten rid of the other two."

"You didn't throw the stuff out?" Neil asked, agonized.

"I didn't want to look at it. But . . ." She put her cup of tea to one side and went across the room to an old rolltop desk in the corner.

Neil couldn't take his eyes off her as she fiddled with the key and rolled up the flap of the desk to reveal a line of pigeonholes stuffed with papers. She started pulling out envelopes and peering at them, only to stuff them back in again. Neil was almost ready to give up when she turned back to him with an envelope in her hand. She was smiling triumphantly. "Here it is."

She handed it to Neil — a stiff, white envelope with the Kennel Club logo on it. It hadn't even been opened. "Go on," Mrs. Atkinson said. "Part of what's in there is yours."

Neil tore open the envelope to look at the documents inside. Emily came to look over his shoulder, and the two dogs pushed forward curiously.

Inside the envelope were the registration documents and pedigrees for three puppies. Neil put to one side the ones that belonged to the little female that died. "But which is which?" he asked Mrs. Atkinson, the sheets for the other two puppies in each hand.

Mrs. Atkinson took the sheets from him and read them carefully. "Your dog seems to be the one with the most white on him," she said. "He's the one that looked most like Betsy." She handed one set of documents back to him. "There you are."

Neil pored greedily over the registration certificate. This was the end of his search and the proof that he had always been right when he said that Sam was a pedigreed dog. It meant a lot, not just to Sam, but to Jake and the rest of the puppies in Delilah's litter, who could be registered now.

Then he saw something that made him look up, mouth open. "Em . . ." he began.

"What's the matter?"

"Look at that." He pushed the certificate under Emily's nose. "Look — the name. Isn't it weird that Sam's original name was Jake?"

CHAPTER NINE

The heavy rain had eased off by the time Neil and Emily said good-bye to Mrs. Atkinson.

"We'll come and see you again," Emily promised. "And we'll bring the dogs to see you, too."

Mrs. Atkinson stood on the step and bent down to pat both dogs as if she couldn't bear to let them go. Neil thought she looked much happier now. He could see how much she loved dogs and that made him feel kinder toward her.

"For sure, we will," he said. "We'll come whenever we can."

They said good-bye and set off up the road toward the old station. When Neil looked back, Mrs. Atkinson was still standing in her doorway, watching them until they were nearly out of sight. He turned and waved, and she waved back to him.

"She must have been really lonely all this time," said Emily. "I think it was a relief to get it all off her chest. She'll be happier now, don't you think?"

"What? Oh, yeah, sure." Neil had other things on his mind. As he walked, he was turning the envelope over and over in his hands. Now that he had actually seen Sam's registration certificate, he could hardly believe it was true. He grinned down at Sam, who was padding quietly along beside him. "I always said you were a star!"

Sam looked up, and Neil was sure he returned the grin.

"Just wait till I show Dad!" Neil said.

"And Jane Hammond," Emily added. "She'll have to tell the people who bought the other puppies. And you'll have to see about registering Jake."

"And give Jim Brewster Skip's papers." Neil had offered to do that for the old lady, and the other certificate and pedigree were in the envelope along with Sam's. "He'll be pretty happy, too."

"I hope he goes to visit Mrs. Atkinson," said Emily. "It'll be nice for her to see Skip as well."

Neil wondered at first if Jim Brewster would see it that way, but he was sure that if he and Emily explained how sorry Mrs. Atkinson was, he would understand and let her make friends with Skip.

Although the rain had almost stopped when they

left Mrs. Atkinson's house, by the time they were walking along the path beside the railroad tracks, it began again, sweeping down in cold curtains from over the hill.

"We'll be soaked by the time we get home," said Neil.

"Better give me the envelope," Emily suggested. "I've got a big pocket inside my jacket."

Neil was a little reluctant to give up his prize, but he handed the envelope over; the papers would be ruined if they got wet. He pulled up the hood of his jacket and thrust his hands deep into his pockets, trying to hide from the rain. They were at least half an hour's walk away from home, and there was nowhere to find shelter along the way. He wondered whether getting wet like this would be bad for Sam.

But Sam was trotting along beside him and seemed less bothered than Neil was by the rain and the muddy road. *Collies are working dogs,* Neil reminded himself. *They're used to being out in all kinds of weather.*

When they reached the river, Neil was surprised to see how much it had risen since they came that way earlier. The muddy water raced along, with bubbles of foam floating on the surface and twigs and other debris caught up in the current. The rocks that usually showed above the surface were almost all covered, with water rushing around them. At the bridge, the current surged just below the planks.

The bridge shook as they stepped onto it. Neil paused in the middle and looked down at the churning water. Harry Grey's fields would be flooded if the water rose much more. And maybe . . .

"Neil!" Emily's sharp cry interrupted his thoughts. "Neil, look!"

Neil followed her finger and looked a short way upstream. A huge branch was being swept down in the current and, before any of them could move, it slammed into the bridge support just below where Neil was standing.

Neil grabbed the handrail to stay on his feet as the bridge swayed alarmingly. The center of it started to dip and creak — water swirled around his ankles. Emily, a few feet farther on, grabbed Sam's collar and headed for the far bank, her feet slipping on the wet planks that had suddenly become a steep ramp.

"Jake!" Neil yelled. "Jake! Here!"

Jake was behind him, whimpering on the edge of the water where it washed over the planks of the bridge. Before Neil could reach him, the bridge started to disintegrate. The planks under his feet were being tugged away by the current and the struts holding them up caved in. Neil tried to pull himself toward Jake using the handrail, but it splintered when he put his weight on it.

He heard Emily shouting his name and Sam barking.

Very slowly, the handrail parted from the rest of

the bridge and Neil fell into the surging water. He grabbed wildly for the bridge support but missed and went under.

For a few seconds, Neil was in shock. The fierce current rolled him over, drove him against the bottom of the river and then carried him on. He couldn't breathe — he couldn't even think.

Then he started to kick out, trying to force himself upward to where he thought the surface was. His head broke out into the air and he trod water, coughing and gasping.

He was being carried quickly downstream. When he could see again, he could make out Emily running along the bank, keeping up with him, and Sam bounding along beside her.

But he couldn't see Jake.

Wildly, Neil looked around him. Rain was still sweeping down, and he could barely see anything. Then he caught sight of Jake a few yards downstream, being carried along just as Neil was. He was holding his head out of the water, but he didn't seem able to swim to the bank.

"Jake! Jake!" Neil yelled.

He couldn't be sure that Jake had heard. He struck out toward him, but his shoes were heavy and his jacket was waterlogged, making him clumsy. He made very little headway. A surge of water washed over his head and he accidentally gulped in a mouthful of it.

I'm going to drown, he thought. *We're both going to drown.*

He kept on trying to reach Jake. Terrified, he saw the little dog's head go under, reappearing a few seconds later. On the bank, Sam was barking furiously, and Emily was yelling for help.

Neil ached all over. Every stroke sapped more of his strength. Then the current drove him against something hard, forcing all the breath out of his body. He grabbed blindly and found he was clinging to a rock.

Jake was not far away. Neil yelled at him again and held out a hand. Jake heard him or saw him and began floundering toward him, but the current was too strong. Neil watched helplessly as his dog was carried farther away from him.

He managed to kick his shoes off and began to wriggle out of his jacket. He would swim better without them and make one last effort to reach Jake.

Then he saw Sam suddenly launch himself from the bank and start swimming strongly across the current.

Neil wanted to shout, "No!" He knew what a risk Sam was taking.

Jake was weakening.

Neil kept losing sight of him as the little dog's head kept dipping under.

Then Sam reached his son. The two dogs' heads showed black above the water. Sam had Jake by the scruff of the neck, but they were being swept farther away from Neil every second. He guessed he could not reach them now if he tried.

It was all up to Sam.

Through the rain and the surging water it was hard to see what was happening, but Neil realized that gradually Sam and Jake were getting closer to the bank. "Go on! You can do it!" he cried.

Emily had waded out into the river and was standing waist deep, reaching out to the dogs as they came closer. Neil saw her take one more step forward. She looked like she would tip over, but then, with Jake in her arms, she staggered back to safety.

Sam found his feet and floundered through the shallows. But as he began to climb up the bank he seemed to fall, his back half still in the water. He scrabbled with his front feet, trying to get up, and then lay still.

Neil froze. He felt sick.

He let go of the rock. He felt the force of the river, but without his heavy clothes he could fight against it. He had to get to Sam. He struck out across the current and, within a dozen strokes, he managed to stand and splash to the bank.

Emily was pulling Sam clear of the water as Neil came pounding up. Tears streamed down her cheeks as she looked up at him.

Neil flung himself down on the bank beside Sam. Water ran off the dog's coat, plastering it to his body. His eyes were closed. A little water and foam trickled from his mouth.

"Sam! Sam!" Neil said frantically. "Wake up! You did it, boy! You saved Jake!"

Sam lay still.

Neil felt for his heartbeat but could not find it. He could hear Emily's sobs, and Jake whimpering somewhere nearby.

He put his arms around Sam, half lifting him. "Sam! Come on, boy — wake up!"

But he knew that Sam would never wake up again.

Neil buried his face in his friend's sodden fur and listened to the rain hissing down all around them.

CHAPTER TEN

"**M**om," said Emily, "I think you should call everyone and cancel the party."

Sun shone through the kitchen window as Carole Parker served scrambled eggs. The previous day's storm had vanished completely. Emily's birthday morning was warm and bright, but Neil felt sick and miserable.

He'd been preparing himself to put his sadness aside and make Emily's birthday a day to remember. He had never imagined that Sam would be dead already.

"Are you sure, Emily?" he heard his mother ask.

"It just doesn't seem right," Emily said, "to be enjoying myself, when Sam . . ." Her voice trailed off miserably.

She couldn't forget the evening before.

Emily had run across the fields to Priorsfield Farm for help. Harry Grey had phoned Bob and then gone back with Emily to the river. By the time they reached the farm again, Bob was waiting with the Range Rover.

Soaked to the skin, clutching Sam, Neil insisted on going straight to Mike Turner's, but the vet had only confirmed what everyone already knew. Sam was dead. The effort of rescuing Jake from the river had been too much for his heart. Mike called Sam a hero when he heard the story.

Neil knew it was true.

Sam had saved Jake twice, once from the mongrel on the hillside and once from the river. But it didn't help much when Neil wondered how he was going to face getting up every day, knowing that Sam would never be waiting for him again.

Mike had checked Jake over and told Neil that the younger dog would be fine if he rested for a day or two. At least caring for Jake gave Neil something to think about. He didn't know how he would have managed if Jake had died, too, and left him completely alone.

Carole brought the plates to the table, but no one felt much like breakfast. Sarah didn't even try to eat. She hadn't known how ill Sam was, and when she saw him dead she had cried and cried. Even now her eyes were red from tears.

Jake knew that something was wrong, too, and crouched quietly in his basket with his nose on his paws.

Carole ate a mouthful of scrambled eggs and put her fork down. "Neil, what do you think?" she asked. "About Emily's party?"

"I don't know." Until now, Neil had never thought about canceling the party, and he wasn't sure that he should be the one to decide. "But I think . . . well, remember what Sam was like. Whenever we were having fun, he wanted to join in. He wouldn't want your birthday spoiled, Em."

"It's not the same without him," Emily said.

Just then the doorbell rang and Bob got up to answer it. He came back into the kitchen a moment later with his hands full of letters and packages. "All for you, birthday girl," he said, trying to sound cheerful. "All except this." He squinted at one long, brown envelope. "All I get is a gas bill."

Neil tried to grin at his dad's feeble joke and watched as Emily started to open her packages. She couldn't help brightening up a little as she took off the wrapping paper.

"Neil, look, it's a card from Max and Prince. And a *Time Travelers* video — it's an episode from the new series! It hasn't even been on TV yet."

"Great," said Neil, looking at the picture of his friend Max and the cocker spaniel Prince beaming out from the cover of the video.

"And Grandma and Grandpa Parker have sent a gift certificate for books — oh, and look, a sweater from Grandma Tansley." Emily unfolded a rather large sweater of yellow wool.

"Well," Carole said, looking at her mother's knitting, "I suppose you'll grow into it."

"And a wildlife book from Uncle Jack and Aunt Mary."

Gradually, everyone around the table was starting to cheer up a bit. Then Sarah suddenly said, "I forgot my present!" and bounced out of the kitchen. Neil followed slowly, to get the mobile he had bought in Warren's.

"Happy birthday, Em," he said as he gave it to her.

Emily loved the mobile, as he had hoped she would, and Sarah's present, too — a picture of Fudge, the hamster, that Sarah had painted and put into a frame.

"And this," said Bob, handing Emily a big envelope, "is our present."

Neil exchanged a glance with his mom. *A leopard, huh? How would you get a leopard flat enough to put in an envelope?*

Suddenly, Emily squealed, "It's a leopard! Mom, Dad, it's lovely!"

"What?" said Neil. "Here, let me look at that!"

Emily handed some papers across the table. First was a certificate from a wildlife charity, saying that Emily Parker had officially adopted a leopard cub in a safari park in Africa. There was a booklet of leopard facts and figures. There was a photograph of the leopard playing under a tree, with sunlight dappling its tawny fur and its big soft paws stretched out in a pretend pounce.

"It says her name's Saba!" said Emily. "And she's really mine! That's the best present I've ever had."

Carole was looking smug. "Told you so," she said to Neil.

"We sponsor the leopard," Bob explained, "so she's

properly cared for. It's a way of fund-raising, and Emily will get regular updates of how she's doing."

Emily's eyes were shining. *This is how it should be,* Neil thought. *This is the sort of morning that I want to remember.*

Though he still didn't feel much like it, he made himself eat a few mouthfuls of scrambled egg and some toast. "Come on, Em," he said. "We've still got a lot to do before your party."

Once the kennel work was done, Neil got a shovel and walked alone to the bottom of the yard. He paused for a moment then grimly began digging. Sam's grave was to be beneath his favorite bush, where he had lazed on sunny days for as long as Neil could remember. Neil had refused help from anyone else. This was the last thing that he could do for his friend. Only Jake came with him and sat quietly in the shade of the hedge while Neil worked.

When the grave was ready, Neil walked across the courtyard to Red's Barn, where Sam's body lay. The barn had been named after another special dog who had died bravely when the old barn burned down, and for a moment Neil wished that Sam could have a memorial like that.

Then, as he looked around, he realized that so much of Sam was in King Street that Neil would never set foot in any part of it without remembering him. Sam had been their first ever rescue dog, and he had helped to make the place what it stood for now. Dogs like Sam were what King Street was all about. All of King Street would be his memorial.

Neil went into the barn and knelt down beside the blanket-covered shape on the floor. In a little while, he would call the rest of the family to bury Sam, but this was his last private good-bye.

He folded the blanket back from Sam's face and neck. Sam looked smaller, and Neil couldn't pretend to himself anymore that he was only asleep. He rested a hand on the ruffled hair.

"Good-bye, boy. You were the best. I won't forget you."

Jake came up, nosed briefly at Sam, and then pushed his muzzle up against Neil as if he was trying to comfort him. Neil put an arm around him, and laid the blanket once again over Sam's face.

If he shed a few tears, there was no one there to see.

All the Parkers gathered after lunch beside the grave. Again, Neil refused help. He silently carried the bundle from the barn and laid Sam in the hole he had dug.

Sarah had picked a handful of daisies, which she scattered into the grave. Emily leaned forward and laid down a photograph of Sam, Jake, and Neil taken at Christmas. It seemed so long ago.

Neil couldn't think of anything to do or say, so he filled in the earth and said a last, silent good-bye to

Sam. Sarah started to cry again, very quietly, and Carole hugged her.

When the job was done, Bob said, "There aren't many dogs like Sam. I know it's hard, Neil. But you'll manage somehow. Try to remember the good things."

He rested a hand on Neil's shoulder for a minute, and then retreated up the path toward the house. Carole followed, shepherding Emily and Sarah, to see to the last-minute preparations for the party.

Left alone again except for Jake, Neil wasn't sure that he was going to be able to manage. *Too many people,* he thought. *All saying they're sorry. I won't know what to say.* He knew it would be easier if he could just stay here in the yard, with Sam.

He watched Jake nosing around in the hedge and felt the pain of Sam's loss ease a little. All this would be a lot harder if he didn't have Jake. There were still plans to be made, for all the dog care and training Jake would need if he was to grow up to be as fantastic a dog as his dad.

Neil knew that Sam had given him that. Without Sam, it would be Jake lying there in the grave under the hedge. He knew, too, that it would be a betrayal to Sam and the sacrifice he had made if he didn't work his very hardest for Jake.

"OK, boy," he said aloud. "I'll give it my best shot."

He started as he heard a footstep behind him. Chris Wilson was standing there. Awkwardly,

he said, "Hi, Neil. Your mom told me. I'm really sorry."

Neil took a deep breath. *This is it*, he thought. *This is the toughest part.* "Thanks," he said.

"He was a great dog," said Chris.

Neil nodded. He snapped his fingers at Jake, who trotted to his side. "Let's go. Em'll be waiting."

As he turned away, he glanced back at the bush where Sam was buried and thought he saw, just for a second, the outline of a dog lying under the hedge with his head cocked alertly, waiting to hear his

master's whistle. Then Neil realized that it was just
a trick of sunlight shining through the leaves.

And yet, he thought, *in a way, Sam will always be
here.*

He clapped Chris on the shoulder and walked
back to the house to join in the party.

Be sure to catch the next exciting Puppy Patrol!

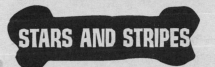

STARS AND STRIPES

Mr. Harman glanced at his watch, then looked at Sue-Ellen. "I hope he's not too late turning up, this boy of yours," he said. "We're losing valuable camera time. Does anyone have any idea how much per minute I'm paying for the use of these studios?"

No one spoke except Wanda, who muttered, "You should have used homegrown talent from the beginning."

Thelma stepped forward. "I have an idea," she said. "I mean, just tell me if you think it's too ridiculous. . . ."

"No, let's have it," Mr. Harman said, while Neil leaned forward to make sure he didn't miss anything.

"It's just that if our friend Max has disappeared

for a while — if he doesn't return for the rest of the day, for example, then maybe you should rethink *Spook Spotting*."

"In what way?" Mr. Harman asked.

"Well, maybe it should be reshot with Abner taking the lead role."

"Oh, Mom!" Abner cried, trying to look surprised and modest at the same time.

"I mean, Abner knows Max's part forward and backward. He could do all the scenes without any trouble. And then when Max comes back from wherever he went, he could play the minor role — the one Abner's got at the moment."

"She has it all worked out!" Emily hissed to Neil.

"And suppose Max doesn't come back?" Mr. Harman asked.

"Well . . ." Thelma looked around. "Maybe we could find some other kid to play the smaller part. It hardly needs someone of Abner's talent to do it." Her eyes lit upon Neil. "Like Max's young friend, for instance. Why couldn't Neil do it? You wanted a Brit in the film, after all."

Neil and Emily both gasped.

But Mr. Harman was shaking his head. "If I needed one, Thelma, I could get any of a dozen young actors with experience."

Sue-Ellen stepped forward. "I think we're all being a bit premature here," she said. "Max has only been missing for a few hours. He'll probably reappear at any moment and then things can go on as normal."

"You're right," Mr. Harman said. "I suggest we continue on with the next scene and then all have a stroll around the place before lunch. Everyone should go to a different area and ask if anyone has seen Max. I'll go to the West Six studio and look there." He consulted his clipboard. "Wanda! Are you ready?" he called.

Wanda was bent over something in the corner and didn't seem to have heard him.

"Wanda!" Mr. Harman called. "You don't have that dog on the set with you again, do you?"

"I do," Wanda said. "Poor little Blossom gets lonely in the dressing room on her own, don't you, my precious?"

"Give me strength," Neil heard Mr. Harman mutter. The director cleared his throat. "Could she go back there, please, Wanda? I want some clear, focused acting from you. I don't get that if you're distracted by having your dog on the set."

"Dressing rooms are dangerous places," Wanda said. "Things disappear and people disappear. It is possible that a dog might disappear."

"At the moment, I *would* really like a dog to disappear from this set," Mr. Harman said in a level voice. He beckoned to Neil. "Please take it away, Neil."

"She has a name!" Wanda put in.

"Please take Blossom back to Wanda's dressing

room, Neil. And then, if you wouldn't mind, could you stay there and dog-sit for half an hour or so — just until we've shot this scene?"

"I'd be happy to," Neil said. He'd taken quite a liking to the tiny Chihuahua and was sure she enjoyed being treated like a dog rather than a toy.

Wanda narrowed her eyes at Neil as she handed him the key to her dressing room. "And I'm warning you, I know exactly what's in that room, boy."

Neil pretended not to hear her. "You stay here," he said to Emily. "Come and tell me as soon as Max turns up."

Emily nodded. "*If* he turns up . . ." she said in a small, worried voice.